this book
belongs to:

weather vane

telescope

lookout

lots of windows!

chimney

sturdy walls

swirly stairs

pirate flag

front door

wooden ladder

mailbox

pretty flowers

To my parents
for raising me to believe that anything is possible.

And to my husband
for making everything possible
(and for building our children's magical "treehouse").

© 2019 Elise Monsour Puckett
The Adventures of Scout and Kit: I Wish I Lived in a Treehouse
First edition, Month 2019

Roly Poly Books, Publishing Company
Christiansburg, VA
EliseMonsourPuckett.com

Editing: Shayla Raquel, ShaylaRaquel.com
Special thanks to Jay Miletsky and Alexa Garvoille
Cover Design & Illustrations: Tessa Riley
Interior Formatting: Elise Monsour Puckett, EliseMonsourPuckett.com

The illustrations in this book were created with Prismacolor Premier pencils on watercolor paper.
Text set in Adobe InDesign.

ISBN 978-0-9994391-1-1

THE ADVENTURES OF
Scout & Kit

I WISH I LIVED in a TREEHOUSE

By: Elise Monsour Puckett

Illustrated by: Tessa Riley

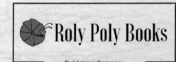

Roly Poly Books

Publishing Company

I wish I lived in a treehouse,
Atop a big ole tree.
My home would be my castle—
What a kingdom it would be!

Daddy and I will build it BIG,
With lots of little nooks
To soar up high into the sky
And hold my favorite books.

It'll have a *swirly-whirly* slide
And a ladder made of rope.

A wooden bridge that swings and sways
(But not too much, I hope!).

A tire swing and a lookout,
A pirate flag and more.

A compass and a telescope,
And yes! My own trap door.

We'll play games like hide-and-seek
And have tea parties for Kit.
Catch fireflies in mason jars,
So our house will be well lit.

Uh-o!

We'll make MIGHTY swords out of sticks
And magic wands that go poof!
One wrong spell with these twigs,
And a goat's up on the roof.

There'd be acorns and inchworms
And birds chirping a song.
They'll hang about our treehouse,
While we try to sing along.

We'll look down from the treetop
To the backyard fields below,
Where seas of dandelion puffs
Give a million wishes to blow.

What if it had a drawbridge,
A moat, and gators that bop?
But my mommy might think
That's a bit over-the-top.

Chomp!

We'll look beyond the branches
At cloud shapes in the sky.
We'll daydream, point, and giggle
At the creatures floating by.

On rainy days, we won't worry,
For that's how rainbows begin.
We'll wear our yellow raincoats
And find puddles to jump in.

Our families will live there too,
And we'll laugh and play all day
Among the cozy branches,
Till the stars come out to play.

When night falls, I will gaze
Upon the planets and the stars
Out into space beyond the moon,
Past Jupiter and Mars.

There's the Milky Way and moonbeams,
Dippers big and small.
A shooting star lights up the sky,
Brighter than them all.

I will close my eyes real tight
And wish upon that star
That my dreams will be so sweet,
And my friends never far.

We'll cast away to Dreamland,
Up the moonbeam we will drift
In a boat with bedsheet sails,
Captain Scout and Skipper Kit.

The wind will be our water,
And the moon will light our trails.
The fish are made of stardust,
And the clouds all look like whales.

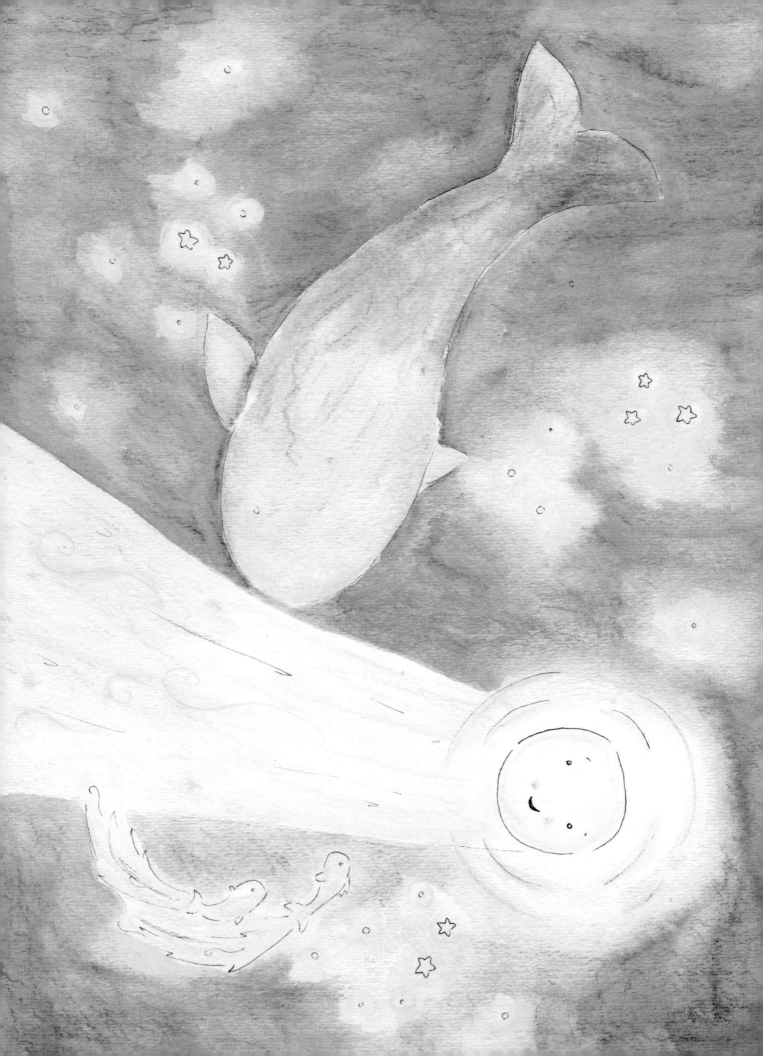

As the night stars fade away,
Down goes our friend the moon.
The early-morning sun comes up,
While the birds all sing a tune.

I give a yawn and rub my eyes,
A swell day it will be.
A new adventure awaits,
high atop our tree.

"Watch the skies for stars that sparkle lightly to and fro.
For these are wishes from the children dreaming down below."

—Judy Monsour, Mother of the Author

Another Scout & Kit book - Collect them all!

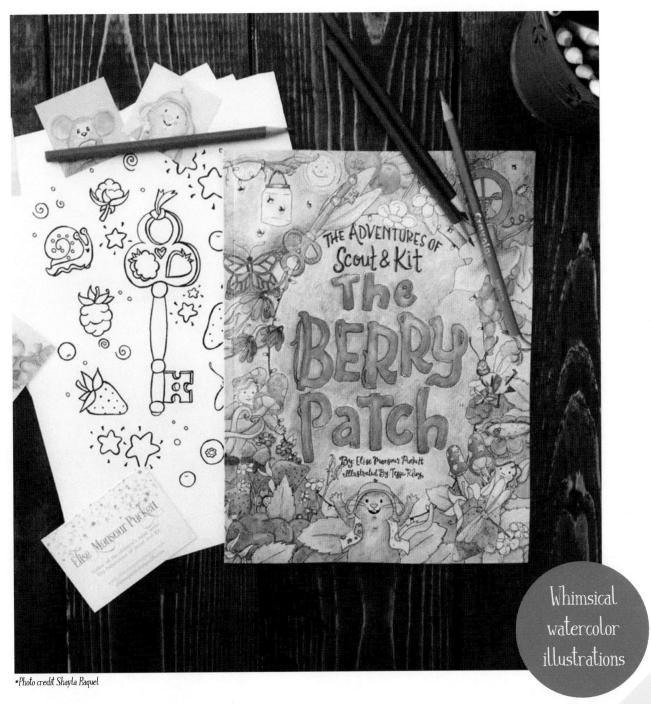

*Photo credit Shayla Raquel

Stickers, coloring pages, bookmarks, teacher lesson plans, plushies, and more!

Go beyond the book!
www.EliseMonsourPuckett.com

Elise takes her tea with a dollop of fresh honey.

About the Author

Elise Monsour Puckett is the author of The Adventures of Scout & Kit series. She is a graduate of Roanoke College with a bachelor's degree in Business Administration. Elise is a writer, author, poet, and storyteller (to her children). She grew up in the little town of Salem, Virginia, and now lives nestled in the foothills of the Appalachian Mountains.

Elise is happily married to a spitfire redhead and is the mother of two beautiful, silly children with great, big imaginations! She gets her inspiration from her children, nature, her inventive father, and her mother, whose dream is to write children's books and poetry.

In her children's playroom is where she does most of her writing, but Elise also enjoys creating her stories while sitting on a picnic blanket outside on a beautiful summer day, and while watching her children catch lightning bugs on sweet summer nights.

It is Elise's dream that her stories bring smiles to the faces of children everywhere and sprinkle each child's day with a little bit of magic when reading her books.

About the Illustrator

Tessa Riley is the talented illustrator behind The Adventures of Scout and Kit children's book series. The whimsical details in her art are one of the many reasons Elise handpicked her to illustrate these magical books.

Born in Georgia, Tessa then moved to Missouri, where she spent ten years of her childhood. She now lives in Afton, Virginia, Blacksburg, Virginia, and is a Virginia Tech graduate with a bachelor's degree in Visual Communication Design and a minor Art History.

Tessa loves the outdoors and hiking with her dog, Roadie. She also enjoys running cross-country and is a former track athlete for Virginia Tech. One of Tessa's passions is traveling and seeking inspiration for her watercolor illustrations while visiting new faraway places.

For more information about Elise Monsour Puckett and her books, please visit EliseMonsourPuckett.com

Made in the USA
Monee, IL
27 November 2019